This book belongs to:

....

....

....

Retold by Gaby Goldsack
Illustrated by Emma Lake (Advocate)
Designed by Jester Designs

Language consultant: Betty Root

ISBN 1-40544-363-4

This is a Parragon Publishing Book
First published in 2004

Parragon Publishing
Queen Street House
4 Queen Street
Bath, BA1 1HE, UK

p

Little
Red Riding
Hood

Helping Your Child Read

Learning to read is an exciting challenge for most children. From a very early age, sharing storybooks with children, talking about the pictures, and guessing what might happen next are all very important parts of the reading experience.

Sharing reading

Set aside a regular quiet time to share reading with younger children, or to be on hand to encourage older children as they develop into independent readers.

First Readers are intended to encourage and support the early stages of learning to read. They present much-loved tales that children will enjoy hearing again and again. Familiarity helps children identify some of the words and phrases.

When you feel that your child is ready to move on a little, encourage them to join in so that you read the story aloud together. Always pause to talk about the pictures. The easy-to-read speech bubbles in **First Readers** provide an excellent "joining-in" activity. The bright, clear illustrations and matching text will help children understand the story.

Building confidence

In time, children will want to read *to* you. When this happens, be patient and give continual praise. They may not read all the words correctly, but children's substitutions are often good guesses.

The repetition in each book is particularly helpful for building confidence. If your child cannot read a particular word, go back to the beginning of the sentence and read it together so the meaning is not lost. Most important, do not continue if your child is tired or just needs a break.

Reading alone

The next step is to ask your child to read alone. Try to be available to give help and support. Remember to give lots of encouragement and praise.

Along with other simple stories, **First Readers** will ensure reading is an enjoyable and rewarding experience.

Once upon a time there was a little girl.
She wore a red hood and cape.
Everyone called her Little Red
Riding Hood.

One day Little Red Riding Hood's
mother said,

"Grandma is sick. Take her this
basket of food."

Little Red Riding Hood's grandma
lived on the other side
of the wood.

I'm going to Grandma's house!

Little Red Riding Hood walked through
the wood toward her grandma's house.

She did not see a hungry wolf
watching her.

The hungry wolf jumped out in front of
Little Red Riding Hood.

"Where are you going?" he asked.

"I'm taking this basket of food to
Grandma who is sick," said
Little Red Riding Hood.

To Grandma's house.

13

"Where does your grandma live?" asked the wolf.

"She lives in a house on the other side of the wood." said Little Red Riding Hood.

The hungry wolf smiled.

Why don't you pick some flowers?

"Why don't you pick flowers for your grandma?" he said.

"What a great idea," said Little Red Riding Hood.

What a great idea.

Little Red Riding Hood put down her basket to pick some flowers.

The hungry wolf smiled.
Then he ran off to Grandma's house.

When he got there, the hungry wolf ate Grandma in one big gulp.

But he was still hungry!

The hungry wolf put on Grandma's
cap and glasses. Then he got into
Grandma's bed and waited for
Little Red Riding Hood.

He did not have to wait long.
Little Red Riding Hood walked in.

"Hello, Grandma," said Little Red
Riding Hood. Then she stopped and
looked.

Hello, Grandma!

"Grandma, what big eyes you have!"
said Little Red Riding Hood.

"All the better to see you with," said
the hungry wolf.

"Grandma, what big ears you have!" said Little Red Riding Hood.

"All the better to hear you with," said the hungry wolf.

"Grandma, what big teeth you have!" said Little Red Riding Hood.

"All the better to eat you with," said the hungry wolf.

Little Red Riding Hood screamed.

Suddenly, the hungry wolf jumped out of bed and...

...ate Little Red Riding Hood in one big gulp!

Now the wolf was not hungry any more. He was very full. He lay on Grandma's bed and fell asleep.

In the wood, a woodcutter heard Little Red Riding Hood scream.

He ran into the house. He saw the wolf asleep on Grandma's bed and...

...killed it with his ax!

"Let us out!" cried Little Red Riding
Hood and Grandma from inside the
wolf's belly.

Stay for tea!

The woodcutter cut open the wolf's belly. Out jumped Little Red Riding Hood and Grandma.

Grandma was so pleased to be saved that she invited the woodcutter to tea!

Read and Say

How many of these words can you say?
The pictures will help you. Look back in
your book and see if you can find the
words in the story.

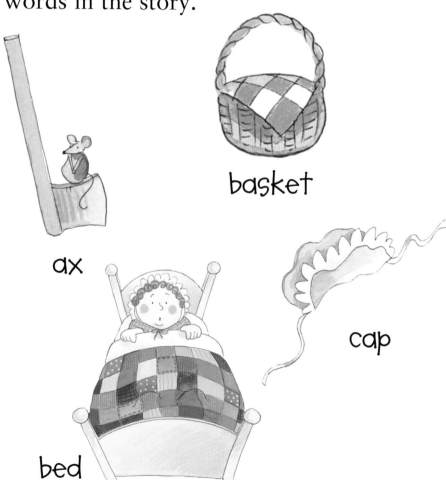

basket

ax

cap

bed

ears

flowers

eyes

glasses

food

Grandma

Titles in this series:

Beauty and the Beast
Chicken-Licken
Cinderella
The Gingerbread Man
Goldilocks and the Three Bears
Hansel and Gretel
Little Red Riding Hood
Sleeping Beauty
Snow White and the Seven Dwarfs
The Three Billy Goats Gruff
The Three Little Pigs
The Ugly Duckling